IAN WHYBROW
ILLUSTRATED BY TONY ROSS

Hodder
Children's
Books

HODDER CHILDREN'S BOOKS

First published in Great Britain in 2000 by Hodder Children's Books
This edition published in 2016 by Hodder and Stoughton

15

A CIP catalogue record for this book
is available from the British Library.

ISBN 978 1444 93576 9

Printed and bound in Great Britain
by Clays Ltd, St Ives plc

The paper and board used in this book
are made from wood from responsible sources

Hodder Children's Books
An imprint of
Hachette Children's Group
Part of Hodder and Stoughton
Carmelite House
50 Victoria Embankment
London EC4Y 0DZ

An Hachette UK Company
www.hachette.co.uk

www.hachettechildrens.co.uk

My Best Friend

The first time my best friend Gary came to our place, it was a *disaster*. I knew it would be. Accidents seem to happen when Gary's about.

Dad was on early turn at work, so he was home too. Boy, was he in a bad mood! Gary and I had just started our tea. In marched Dad from the bathroom.

3

He was furious, waving a towel with black handprints on it. "Henry!" he said. "Look at the state of this!" I knew what was coming, so I tried to calm things down. I said, "Hi Dad, I don't think you've met Gary before."

Gary thought he'd better explain about the towel and say sorry. He'd been fiddling about with an engine, and got a bit of oil on his fingers.

The trouble was, he had just been showing me how he could squeeze a whole chocolate biscuit into his mouth in one go. Out came this huge shower of crumbs.

4

All Dad could hear Gary say was, "WOFF BOFFF KOFFFF!"

Dad's jaw fell open, but no sound came out. He got even more boiled-looking.

That made Gary go all flustered and he tried to swallow some tea to make a bit more room to talk. The tea was boiling hot! He went, "AHHH!" and started jumping about like a firecracker.

Mum came in to see hot tea flying all over the sandwiches and Gary going mad, juggling with the cup to stop it from breaking. That was a shame. Because the cup smashed anyway and he got his hand scalded as well!

There was jam on the wall, jam on the photo of Mum and Dad getting married, jam on the geranium and jam right down Dad's nice clean shirt.

Mum and Dad had a right go at me after Gary went home.

Dad yelled, "We bring you up nicely and what do we get for it?"

"Jam up the wall!" yelled Mum.

Dad said, "Why can't you have a nice normal friend, instead of a walking accident?"

To be fair, it wasn't really Gary that upset Dad. It was his job, at

 Foodico, the supermarket. Mr Bird, the manager, was retiring, and

Dad and the other deputy manager, Dennis Smart, were both after his job. Dad was shy and hard-working.

Mr Smart was loud and flashy. He was always sucking up to Mr Bird. So Dad reckoned that Mr Smart would get the job, and that the first thing he'd do would be to give Dad the sack.

Dad was especially worried about the big charity event that was coming up. Foodico sponsors one every year.

"This year, it's a big go-kart race at Belmont Park," he said. "Anyone who raises more than £200 for charity can enter a driver. All sorts of companies are entering. But our branch of Foodico raised £500 and so we're entering *two* drivers. And Mr Bird thinks it would be a good idea if his two deputies competed."

I could tell Dad was nervous enough about entering a go-kart race. But it would be even worse having to race Mr Smart for the manager's job *and* for the winner's shield!

As usual, Mr Smart was a tricky bloke to beat, because he didn't play by the rules. It wasn't long before I saw for myself just how *sneaky* he could be.

Trouble at Foodico

After school on Monday, Gary and I nipped into Foodico to pick up a few bits and pieces for Mum. She wanted vanilla essence, so I took  the basket and headed for the "Home Baking" section. Gary went to "Confectionery" to pick up this special bar of chocolate.

"Meet you at the checkout," I said.

A couple of minutes later, I heard a sound like an avalanche, followed by a man's voice shouting, "Hold it right there, Sunshine!"

I went to see what had happened (me and a crowd of customers) and found Gary rubbing his head and looking a bit pale. A pyramid of pineapple tins had collapsed and fallen into the aisle, right where he was walking. And who watched it all happen? Mr Smart, of course.

"Look what you've done!"
boomed Mr Smart. "You could have
caused someone a real injury! *And*
 you've been pinching
chocolate!" He snatched
the bar out of Gary's hand.
"No I'm not! I was
collecting it for—"
"Where's your basket then?" Mr
Smart demanded.

I was going to say I had it but
just at that moment, Dad came
rushing over. After Dad's last
meeting with Gary, I feared the
worst. But all Dad said was, "It's all
right, Mr Smart. He's with my
Henry. If Gary says it was an
accident, I'm quite sure it was."

"It was, Mr Wilson," Gary
explained. "I was just walking past
all these tins and I could see they
were going to fall. So I held my
hands up like this . . ." (He held
them high so everyone could see.)
"But there were too many of them.
They fell right on my head."

Dad just said, "I hope you didn't hurt yourself." I was amazed! But I didn't realize then that Dad had seen who had stacked that shaky pyramid – none other than Mr Dennis Smart himself!

Just then, the manager, Mr Bird, arrived. Straight away, Mr Smart took him aside and gave him his side of what had happened. Dad set about picking up the tins and telling the customers that there was nothing to worry about. Gary and I helped.

When Mr Smart had finished explaining, the manager gave Gary a dirty look and started to tick him off. I thought, "Oh no, we've had it now!" Dad doesn't like to argue, but there was no way he was going to let Gary be blamed for something that was Dennis Smart's fault. He told the manager that Gary had done nothing wrong and that he deserved an apology.

"Here here!" said an old gent who was still hanging around. And suddenly other shoppers joined in.

"Yes, he wasn't doing any harm! He was trying to help."

"Be fair!"

Mr Smart was hopping mad, but what could he do? In the end, the manager had to agree with Dad, so Mr Smart had to put on a sickly smile, pat Gary on the head and say, "Ah well. Just a little misunderstanding. No hard feelings, eh?"

But there were. Some *very* hard feelings. After that, Mr Smart did everything he could to give Dad a hard time.

Gary Wants to Help

 Gary was really grateful to Dad for sticking up for him.

"He always tries to be fair," I told him. "It's just that when you first met him, he was in a bad mood." I told him all about the charity go-kart race and how Mr Smart was trying to make Dad look bad, so he could get the manager's job.

"Well, one good turn deserves another!" said Gary. "He'll want to practise, won't he? What about coming along to Sweet Dreams?"

I didn't tell you that Gary's dad works at Sweet Dreams Amusement Park, did I? He runs Demon Racers which just happens to be the go-kart track! So Gary knows tons of stuff about go-kart engines and driving.

"I thought Sweet Dreams was closed until Easter," I said.

"Most of the rides are, but they hire out the go-kart track to a local club at the weekend. Tell your dad about it. If he'd like to do some practising there, I could ask mine to give him a few tips."

"It's a great idea, Gary," I said. "But I'd better not mention it came from you. Somehow I think you'd better keep away from Dad for a while. Just to be on the safe side. In case there are any more little accidents!"

Dad jumped at the chance to practise at Sweet Dreams. Gary and I were dying to see how he was getting on.

But Dad wasn't keen on having any spectators. So Gary said, "Ask your mum if you can come and spend the day with me. My dad's got his little office overlooking the track. He won't mind if we keep out of sight in there and watch your dad out of the window."

Poor old Dad. He was all alone on the track, apart from Reg, who worked for Gary's dad. Reg wasn't a lot of help. He just pointed out the controls and let Dad get on with it.

Talk about slow and steady! Dad was like a snail, and wobbling all over the place. "Don't go so heavy on the steering, Mr W!" Gary muttered, misting up the window.

After a couple more laps, Dad was no quicker, really, but he was a bit straighter. Gary whispered, "Bit more speed now, Mr W."

Suddenly there was a much louder voice booming across the park. It nearly made us jump. "Move it, Wilson! Give it some welly!"

It was Mr Smart, looking all flash in a red racing overall, with a matching hanky tied round his neck.

"What's *he* doing here?" I hissed.

"Must belong to the club that hires the track!" replied Gary.

He must have made my dad jump too. He hit the brake too hard, skidded, spun the back end right round and spluttered to a stop.

"Now you've killed your engine!" yelled Mr Smart. "You're going to need a bit more bottle if you're going to be any good at this game.

Want to see it done properly? Watch the expert!" He tightened the strap on his helmet, hopped into his go-kart, started up, revved the engine – *VRRRM VRRRM!* Then he screamed off down the track.

"What a show-off!" said Gary. "But look at him *go!*"

"Dad hasn't got a chance!" I moaned.

"Don't worry, mate, he needs more practice, that's all," said Gary. "Smartypants just *thinks* he's brilliant. How long is it before the race?"

"Only two weeks," I replied gloomily.

"Blimey! We're going to have to think of a plan! And quickly," said Gary.

The Demon Racer's Offer

Normally I look forward to Saturday tea, but not that Saturday. Dad was looking dead miserable. Mum asked, "How did you get on at the racetrack?"

"Pretty hopeless," sighed Dad. "Dennis Smart turned up. First he raced the pants off me. Then he reminded me that they close Sweet Dreams in the evenings, which means he can carry on practising and I can't."

"How come?" I asked.

"Because he's talked Mr Bird into changing our duties. I'm on afternoon shift for the next two weekends and he's working evenings! Then he gave me another  bit of bad news. Lord Hawkins, the big chief of Foodico, is coming to present the champion's shield.

He's going to be interviewing

 Dennis and me for the manager's job. According to Dennis, Lord Hawkins is batty about go-karting. He's bound to think that the winner ought to get the promotion!"

"Nonsense! He's after a manager, not a racing driver!" Mum said.

"The point is," replied Dad, "if you can't show who's boss in a go-kart, you're not going to be much good as boss of a supermarket, are you?"

*

"Dad really needs your help," I said to Gary next day at school. I explained the new problem. "Is it still OK if I ask him if you can help us out?"

Gary smiled. "Not just yet, mate. I've got an idea that just might work. Let me talk to *my* dad first."

It was dark by the time Dad got home on Tuesday. He was really fed up. A customer had been seen on camera stealing a bottle of whisky. Dad had tried to catch the man but he was too fast for him and ran off.

Mr Bird had made a comment about how lucky the man was that Dennis Smart wasn't on duty; he'd have been nippy enough to stop him.

"You can imagine just how Dennis looked when he heard!" Dad groaned. "Ooh, what I'd give to wipe that smug grin off his face in the charity shield race! But when am I ever going to get any practice?"

"You could go down to Sweet Dreams any night and have a go on the Demon Racer track," I suggested, all innocent.

"Don't be daft," Dad said. "Sweet Dreams doesn't open at night."

"I think they might do, if you ask them. Gary says you should call up a bloke called Lightning who works there. Tell him you're a friend of Gary Mason's."

Dad groaned. "What would *Gary* know about it? Still, it's not a bad idea. I need all the help I can get."

 So Dad rang "Lightning". What he didn't know was that "Lightning" was really Gary's dad, and I certainly didn't tell him!

Gary's dad was happy to stay on at the racetrack after work. "But the plan is that I disguise myself as Dad and do the training myself!

Dad will stay in the office," Gary told me on the quiet. "He thinks it'll be a good laugh to have me pretending to be him. We can call him any time we need him, but he's not worried. As long as we know what we're doing. And the truth is, I know loads more about go-karting than he does, anyway!"

So that was that. Next night, we'd all be at Sweet Dreams after dark – Dad and me (I'd talked him into letting me watch). And Gary, otherwise known as "Lightning".

Sweet Dreams at Night

Dad was just as excited about being at Sweet Dreams again as I was.

We'd just got inside the main gate when a short man with a black beard, wearing a big leather jacket and sunglasses, suddenly appeared.

He held out his hand
and said in a deep,
gruff voice,
"Evening, Guv.
You must be Mr
Wilson. My name's
Lightning. Gary's told
me a lot about you."

Dad looked a bit puzzled. "How
do you know young Gary?"

"Er . . . I'm a friend of the family.
He's a good lad. He'll be at home
now, studying," growled "Lightning".

Gary was overdoing it a bit, but
Dad didn't notice. He was too keen
to get on the racetrack. He just said,
"That's where Henry ought to be
right now, I suppose."

Gary ignored that. He growled, "Mustn't waste time nattering – let's get a move on. Just a mo', mate." He nipped ahead and disappeared for a few seconds. Then he must have pulled a lever, because there was the track, lit up like a Christmas tree. Three go-karts were waiting at the start line.

"You take SD11, Henry," "Lightning" said to me.

Dad spluttered, "Do you think that's a good idea? I mean, Henry's only a lad, and—"

"Lightning" cut in. "If other people race against you, you'll feel the pressure a bit more. It'll be good training for the big race. All right?"

Dad nodded quietly, and Gary went on, "Your dad's going to have to learn to get past us two, right? And Mr W, you take SD3 – she's the nippy one, she is. And I'll take old SD7. Now then, helmets on, nice and tight.

"First off, everybody just follow me nice and steady, and see if you can get a clean line round the corners. Nothing fast, nothing fancy. Ready?"

Off we went, Gary in front, then Dad, then me. After four laps, Gary went a bit faster. Dad wobbled, so

did I. The steering wheel pulled your arms all over the place. Then we started to get the hang of it.

We did ten laps, then Gary waved his right arm up and down as a signal for us to stop.

"You're doing great, lads!" he smiled. "Now watch while I do a tail spin." He revved up, roared along the straight and suddenly flipped the back right round.

Afterwards, he said, "Your turn now. You've got a couple of nice little karts there. Remember, they're light but they've got powerful engines. All you've got to do is hit the brake, and give the wheel a tickle, right? Then round she goes. Now, Henry, you go first, my son!"

I tried to remember what Gary said. I put my foot down and felt my head flip back as my kart shot off like a bullet. I gripped the wheel and I gathered speed along the straight. The corner came up much too fast. I panicked. Down with my foot, much too hard! WHEEEEE! I closed my eyes and . . . I'd done it!

My heart was pounding as I punched the air.

"You two make it look so easy!" said Dad nervously.

"Everything's easy when you know how, Mr W," said Gary. "Off you go then. Get your foot down."

I don't know who was more surprised when Dad got it right first time – him or me.

Picking up Speed

The two weeks before the race flew by. Every day, Dad had to go into work and listen to Mr Smart boasting about what a brilliant driver he was. And every night, he and I went along to the Sweet Dreams track. Bit by bit, Gary helped him get his confidence up. Dad was doing less braking, he could recover from the odd knock, and bit by bit, his cornering improved quite a lot.

Being good at cornering was important for our race plan. Dad was great as long as he was following "Lightning". If he was out in front on his own, he couldn't keep up his concentration. He went all wobbly, so what could we do?

It was Gary's dad who came up with the answer. He persuaded his boss at Sweet Dreams to sponsor a kart for the race. "After all," he grinned, "it's for a good cause and it's good publicity for us. Gary can do the driving for us, disguised as me! Wah ha ha! What a laugh!"

So that was that. Gary, alias "Lightning", explained the race plan to Dad. He would keep ahead of Dad and gradually work his way past the other racers. If Smartypants was leading, they'd go past him in the last couple of laps, then Dad would have to fight it out with Lightning for the finishing line.

"I wouldn't feel bad about losing to Lightning," said Dad. "As long as I get to the chequered flag before Dennis Smart."

On the day of the
race, Dad was so
shaky he
couldn't even
drink his cup of
tea properly.

"They'll all be there," he
said to Mum. "All the top people
from Foodico Head Office. I just
hope I can give our Mr Smart a bit
of a run for his money without
making too much of a charley of
myself. Now where's Lightning? He
should be here by now!"

"Don't worry, Dad," I said,
though I was a bit worried myself. I
wondered what Gary's disguise
would look like in daylight.

Belmont Park was echoing to a sound like angry wasps as go-kart engines revved while a commentator's voice crackled over the loudspeakers. Dad was strapped into his go-kart, ready for a couple of practice laps before the off. Mum and I had found a good place to stand, just across from the line that was the start and the finish. I told Mum I'd go and look for him.

"Well hurry up, they'll be starting soon!" said Mum.

"Don't worry, there's at least five minutes," I called as I pushed into the crowd and out of sight.

Five minutes! I dashed to the changing room. Gary was waiting by the door with his arm in a sling!

"You know me, mate," he shrugged. "An accident waiting to happen. I slipped on a patch of oil, and dislocated my shoulder. There's no way I can drive now, so quick, get this lot on! You'll have to drive SD7!"

"ME?"

"Go on, you know what to do!" he said.

My heart was pounding like a drum. But who else was going to help Dad win? While I was scrambling into Gary's racing gear, he kept on talking. "DL13 is all nicely set for Mr W. I ran through the checks myself. You'll have to do your own. Can you remember how?"

I nodded.

In two minutes I had all my racing gear on and I was squeezing my head into my helmet.

 I snapped shut the dark visor on my helmet so nobody could recognize me, and ran like mad towards the start-line.

I whipped open the engine cover. What was I looking for? Chain-drive nice and firm? Check. Dogs and sprockets well oiled?

Check. Air and gas mixture set for high revs? Check. Tyre pressures and suspension? Check.

Suddenly the announcement came over the loudspeakers. "And now, ladies and gentlemen, the race you've all been waiting for – the Foodico Charity Shield. We've got nineteen starters – all tuned up and ready to go!"

A voice louder than the revving of engines came through to me. It was Dennis Smart's. He was kicking the back wheel of DL13 and shouting to Dad above the general noise.

"Where on earth did you dig up that terrible old heap?" His own kart was a gleaming red machine with racing stripes. "Still, all the best, old chap. You're going to need it!"

The Race

The announcement went on. "My name is Lord Hawkins and I'm the founder of Foodico. I'm proud to say that among our starters today, we have managers and deputies from Foodico stores all over the country." (There was a big cheer.) "We also have one late entry, a mystery driver.

He wishes to keep his name a secret, but I understand that he is being sponsored by Sweet Dreams Amusement Park.

"This is a testing twenty-five lap race. The winner will be awarded not only this handsome shield inscribed with his name for all time, but a personal cheque from Foodico for £1,000." (More cheers and some gasps, including one from me. I didn't know that!) "And of course, a further cheque for £5,000 will be also donated by Foodico to the splendid charity we are supporting today.

Now, are we ready, gentlemen?"

I had no time for a practice lap. We had what they call a staggered start. We were given a number out of a hat. Mine was twelve – miles back!

I noticed that Mr Smart was about three places in front of me, but I couldn't see Dad at all. I just hoped that he was close enough to see my number so he could hang on to my tail! The starter raised his flag.

VVRRRM VVRRRM – the noise
was deafening. Three-two-one –
OFFFF! Away we went, dust flying
everywhere!

For the first few laps, I was so
wound up, I didn't have a clue what
was happening. Every now and
then, somebody would drift in front,
or spin out of control and EEEK!
You had to slide past somehow.
There seemed to be hundreds

of karts on that track.

My suspension was really sharp, so I could feel every bump and dip. I had to concentrate like mad just to hold my line.

By lap five I'd calmed down enough to be able to take a proper look for Dad. I glanced over my shoulder. There he was, hanging on

 to my tail! By lap ten I felt like the king of the road! With Dad sticking like glue, I started passing people.

Weaving and swerving I was watching for the red colours of Smartypants – and there he was, running smoothly, bullying his way to the front. He was like a rocket on the straight sections. We slid, we cut corners, we tried our best to keep our feet off our brakes.

We had to be patient. It was a long race and there were times I nearly gave up hope of catching the red racer. He was fearless.

When there were just four laps to go and just two cars between me and Mr Smart, I decided it was now or never. "Hold on, Dad!" I yelled, wishing he could hear me.

I tried to remember Gary's advice. "Just get in front of him and hold him up at the corners. Try and get him to do something daft." It was time to get some speed up.

Coming down the back straight, I got past Number Three, and I started planning how I would cut past Number Two as he went into the tight left-hander. The trouble was, he bottled out, braked too soon and spun right round in front of me!

I jammed my foot down on the throttle, steered hard right – and felt the back end drifting. I turned the wheel into the skid, just the way Gary taught me – and *just* managed to skim round him.

I was right behind the red car now. "OK Mr Smart, watch this kart!" I said to myself. I knew he had an excellent machine and for a few seconds I thought he would be too much for me. Then with just three bends left, his cornering let him down. He slowed at the right-hander and cut across to keep me out. I slipped down into third gear with the engine whining, down into second as I came into the corner, then up again into fourth as the kart  started into the straight.

Being so light, I pushed my speed up that way – and sailed outside him into the lead – but only just. I couldn't take Dad with me. He fell back behind Mr Smart's car and there was a gap opening up.

Next thing I knew, something slammed into my rear wheel and I was spun round and round, off the track – and out of the race.

Once my engine had cut, I could hear the commentator. "And Dennis Smart in the red car beats Rupert Wilson in DL13 by just over half a lap."

Yesssss!

I don't think I've ever felt worse in my life. All that effort for nothing. That horrible Mr Smart had won. Now he'd be manager and fire Dad. We would have to move. Gary and I would never meet again.

Gary hobbled over to help sort me out almost before I'd come to a stop. We had a look at the damage. The back wheel was practically torn off and the bodywork was a mess.

 "Nah, it's all right, mate," said Gary. "Don't worry, we'll soon fix 'er up! Cor, you did well!"

"He certainly did!" I knew that voice. It belonged to the man who introduced the race. I looked up and saw Lord Hawkins, the boss of Foodico. He had Dad with him.

"May I shake hands with the Mystery Driver?" said Lord Hawkins. "And may I introduce you to the winner of the race, Rupert Wilson."

Dad held out his hand to Gary. "Thanks, Lightning! I couldn't have done it without you! Did you hear?

60

Dennis Smart was disqualified for deliberately barging me!"

I slipped back the dark visor. "Congratulations, Dad!" I smiled.

"Henry!" exclaimed Dad. "What happened to Lightning? Do you mean to say that was you I was following all the way?"

"It was going to be Gary, only he dislocated his shoulder," I said. "We owe it all to him, really." There was a lot of explaining to do.

*

A week later, Lord Hawkins offered Dad the manager's job. "What I want in my managers," he told him at his interview, "is courage, steadiness and fair play. The way you drove in that race showed that those are exactly the qualities you have!"

He also happened to mention that Mr Smart had called Head Office and requested a transfer to another county. "A bit embarrassed, I shouldn't wonder," said Lord Hawkins with a wink.

After school that day, Dad invited Gary round to our house. He took us out to the garage and showed us two fabulous mountain bikes.

"These are for you two," Dad smiled. "I bought these with the winner's cheque – because you two were the real winners. And they're my way of saying sorry to Gary – I completely misjudged you. You're a great kid. And you too, Henry. I'm very proud of you both!"

Gary and I stammered thanks, and then we were off, to try our bikes out.

"Hey, Gary! Take it easy with that shoulder," we heard Dad call. "And drop in at Foodico on your way home. There's a year's supply of chocolate biscuits waiting for you! Don't eat them all at once!"